To Seth, my rainbow monster.
My grandad Tom, who has always taught me that
the pen is mightier than the sword.

First Published by Compass-Publishing UK 2021
ISBN 978-1-913713-66-9

Text © Laura Maclennan, 2021
Illustrations © Kylie Dixon, 2021
Laura author photo © Laura Maclennan, 2021

Typeset by The Book Refinery Ltd
www.thebookrefinery.com

DON'T BE SILLY!

For James + Maggie

#bemoreseth

Laura Maclennan

Written by

Laura Maclennan

Illustrated by

Kylie Dixon

#BEMORESETH

First we've got Red, the shape of a heart.
His muscles and claw feet set him apart.
If you ask him for help he won't run a mile.
Simply says it's 'nee botha' and gives you a smile.

Up next is Orange, a cuddly chap.
No ifs and no buts and that is just that.
Never a one to get stuck in a muddle
but avoids the whole world trying to give him a cuddle.

You don't mess with Yellow — boy, she knows her stuff.
Gives you the chills when she acts hard and tough.
But behind those long lashes and lips you will see
an organised lass who'd invite you for tea.

What Green lacks in words he makes up for in height.
You might, on first glance, get a bit of a fright.
But this gentle giant doesn't do well with rifts.
He'd rather whittle wood to make fanciful gifts.

'Graceful' isn't a word to be used for Blue.
Bless him, he's lush but he's not got a clue.
He'll find what you need whatever the task —
you just don't know where it came from, if anyone asks!

Grab your sunnies for Indigo, her presence blinds a room.
Her light shines upon us, she doesn't 'do' gloom.
Just like with her fabric, feels life can be made.
But remember — don't hurt her, 'cos she'll cast you in shade.

And last, there's Purple, the friendliest yet.
He's defo a character you'll never forget.
His hair makes him stand out yet folk think he's boring.
But he's loyal and kind — a friendship worth exploring.

This book belongs to

Sitting in his garden, just down the street,
was Seth — a young boy who's a pleasure to meet.
Today his smile was as bright as could be,
because his daddy had said, 'Build a house in the tree.'

Seth didn't know quite how he should start.
Then along came Red Monster, the shape of a heart.
Red Monster listened, said he'd help if he could,
and that perhaps Seth could start by finding some wood.

So Seth brought some wood and the tree house took shape.
Red said, 'Now for a hammer, some nails and some tape.'
'Orange Monster can bring those,' said Seth, feeling great.
'No way!' cried Red Monster. 'He's too overweight.'

'DON'T BE SILLY!' answered Seth. 'He's just a bit round.

He'll help get our tree house right off the ground.'

Orange Monster came by with his tools and a song.
He helped make the tree house feel sturdy and strong.
'But we need it up high,' Orange said, with great sorrow.
Said Seth, 'Yellow's got the perfect crane we can borrow.'

'She can't help!' cried Orange. 'Yellow's far too long.'

'DON'T BE SiLLY!' answered Seth.

'Her length makes her strong.'

Yellow Monster arrived with her crane's giant hand,
and lifted the house up away from the land.

Once the task was done,
Yellow gave a big grin.
'Now for a ladder,' she said,
'so that you can climb in.'

'Green Monster can build one,' said Seth. 'That's a plus.'
'Not him!' bellowed Yellow. 'He's so much bigger than us.'

'DON'T BE SiLLY!' said Seth, 'His height isn't bad...
We need him — just wait, he'll make us all glad.'

Green Monster built a ladder that was really quite tall.
'Brilliant!' shrieked Seth. 'Now we won't slip and fall.'
'But you still need windows,' said Green, 'and a door.'
'Don't worry,' said Seth. 'Blue has a big saw.'

'Not him,' muttered Green. 'I don't like his angle.
He doesn't move well and just gets in a tangle.'

'DON'T BE SiLLY!' said Seth. 'He just needs his space.

And he'll do what we need without wrecking the place.'

Blue Monster arrived with a door that was brown,
and cut out a window that gave views of the town.
He said, 'Looks very nice, but you'll be needing a curtain.'
Seth squealed, 'I'll ring Indigo. She'll help, I'm certain.'

'Not her!' pleaded Blue. 'She thinks she's so bright.'

'DON'T BE SILLY!' cried Seth.

'She's really quite a delight.'

Indigo Monster came with her dazzling fabric,
and whipped up some curtains as though she was magic.
'There you are, Seth,' she said, 'but please now be told —
you must decorate in here, so it doesn't feel cold.'

'That's easy,' said Seth. 'Purple Monster will help.'
But he stopped in his tracks as the monsters all yelped.

'NOT HIM!' they all cried. 'He's simply a square.
He's a bit of a bore and he's got weird hair.'

'DON'T BE SILLY!' said Seth. 'He's as kind as they come.

I know where I stand and he'll get the job done.'

Purple Monster arrived with some pictures and rugs.
In a basket he'd brought with him eight big mugs.
Within the blink of an eye the work was all done.
Purple said, 'Now it's time for some juice and some fun.'

Red Monster was shocked; Orange Monster made a face.
Yellow Monster lay down and Green started to pace.
Blue Monster felt wobbly; Indigo went dim.
Seth felt quite cross with the friends around him.

'What's wrong with you all? Being together's not bad!'
Seth shouted, and realised he was getting quite mad.
'We've all worked today. We've all played our part.
We're better together than when we're apart.

'I don't look like you. You don't look like each other.
But I also don't look like my sister or brother.
Please let us stop looking at what's not the same.
Instead, look for more ways to be together again.

'Our differences make us better, let's not be alone.
Each one of us here has a place in my home.
Climb into my tree house and we'll all have a think
About how to be kinder, while enjoying a drink.

'It may seem strange, but please understand —
with some talking and listening, we'll be the happiest band.'
So they all drank some juice, played some games and did find
that life was much better when they chose to be kind.

Seth's tree house was filled with jokes, cake and love,
while a rainbow shone over it high up above.

Suggested Reading Activities

Reading is such a powerful skill for everybody to have, and you can begin at any age. Snuggling up with her children or reading with her class is one of Laura's favourite things to do. Reading develops comprehension skills, vocabulary, imagination and in *Don't Be Silly!*, allows the sharing of important messages about friendship, kindness, tolerance and the power of working together.

Some children find it easier to read than others so here are some ways to make books more accessible:

- Have a designated space and time to share a book together.
- Look at the pictures both in and outside the book and talk about what they mean.
- Read out loud and ask your child questions about what you have read.
- Encourage them to read smaller words and words that repeat, to develop their confidence.
- Take your time to enjoy reading together.

Some questions to ask:

- What shape and colour are the monsters?
- What might the story be about?
- Why does Seth say, 'Don't be silly!' to each monster?
- Why do you think Seth started to feel cross with his friends?
- There are some balloons hidden within the pictures... Can you find them all?

The Seth Challenge

Are you ready to #bemoreseth?

Calling out unkindness: if you see someone being unkind to another person, calling them names because of what they like to play or because of what they look like, tell them to stop. Or get an adult to tell them to stop and to #bemoreseth.

The Rainbow Monsters' Challenge

RED MONSTER — be helpful.

Do helpful things at home or school without being asked. It's kind and it will make you and other people feel great.

ORANGE MONSTER — say thank you.

These two words are so powerful and make such a difference. Write down ten things you are thankful for and make an effort to say thank you to everyone you meet every day.

YELLOW MONSTER — share what makes you special.

Create a poster sharing what makes YOU special. You ARE special and it's important to know why that is.

GREEN MONSTER — tell someone else why they are special.

Write a letter or make a card and send it to someone telling them exactly why they are special to you and to others. Then post it.

BLUE MONSTER — make their day.

Do a random act of kindness. Surprise someone with flowers, tell a joke, make a phone call, sing a song, draw a picture — anything that you know will make them feel warm and fuzzy and special.

INDIGO MONSTER — dance.

Put on your favourite music and dance, dance, dance. This will make you feel happy and you'll pass on that happiness to others.

PURPLE MONSTER — pay it forward.

Every time someone shows you kindness or unkindness, make an extra-special effort to be kind to someone else. Sprinkle kindness around like glitter!

Share your challenge successes on social media using the hashtag #bemoreseth

Where you can find us:

www.instagram.com/bemoreseth

www.facebook.com/bemoreseth and
Facebook Group - Seth and the Rainbow Monsters

www.sethandtherainbowmonsters.com

About the Author

Laura is an experienced teacher, leadership coach, sprinkler of all things positive and magical, and a self-confessed lover of the 80s' power ballad. When not playing with her children or working, Laura can be found sneaking a bar of chocolate on the stairs or reading in her book nook with a nice cup of tea.

Laura grew up experiencing unkindness herself and then went on to teach across the curriculum, particularly drama, and within the Special Educational Needs sector. So she knows only too well how small differences can become large beacons for creating division and sadness. With this in mind, and having had her own children, Laura wanted to create something to teach children from a young age that kindness is stronger than unkindness and has more longevity; that our differences make us better. She also wanted to create a simple reminder of this for children to call upon when needed.

With major 'mam guilt' because she has already written a book for her daughter, Eliza, *Don't Be Silly! Featuring Seth & the Rainbow Monsters* was created for her son, Seth.

Written just before rainbows became forever linked to the incredible NHS, the Rainbow Monsters were born, because real Seth is Laura's 'rainbow baby' – the term used for a baby born after a miscarriage or other devastating baby loss. With imaginary Seth and his colourful monster friends, Laura wanted to honour the colour Seth has brought to her world, as well as to bring brightness and kindness to bedtime stories and classrooms everywhere.

Laura hopes that the message of *Don't Be Silly!* will resonate with all who read it and create a ripple of kindness and acceptance, so that both her children and yours can be exactly who they are born to be, by remembering it's ok to #bemoreseth.

Acknowledgements

While my husband, Brett would love the top spot, I cannot and will not ever be able to thank the 'Dream Team' enough for what they have helped me to create here. From first asking illustrator extraordinaire and Queen of the Mushies, Kylie Dixon if she fancied taking a look at *Don't Be Silly!*, to her putting me in contact with Alexa Tewkesbury, editing genius, and Alexa Whitten, typesetting and publishing maestro, this process has been a dream – and a dream come true! Thank you Alexa T for making my words shinier and for your kindess throughout. Thank you Alexa W for the most beautiful layout, for your guidance, humour and for helping me to believe that I am an author. You each make your jobs look easy but I know it takes great skill and dedication, which you both have in abundance.

Which leaves the third musketeer. Kylie, this book would not be the same without your astonishing ability to take what is in my head and bring it to life on paper. Seth and the Rainbow Monsters became a reality because of you and they will live on in hearts for a very long time! Thank you so much for your honesty, your talent, your dedication, and for being such a massive cheerleader of myself and this colourful, motley crew. I couldn't have done it without you.

Other shoutouts go to Amy and Jenny; thank you for always replying to my voice notes and reminding me that I can. To my lifelong 'Seths', Karen, Jo, Kelly and Jo; thank you for being the treehouses I can always call home. Huge thanks to the incredible members of The Northern Lass Lounge and, of course, Seth and the Rainbow Monsters; you did this too! #bemoreseth WILL be trending one day because of you all and the ripple will begin to make waves.

Last, and by no means ever least, to Brett, Eliza and Seth; thank you, thank you, thank you. You guys bring the rainbows and red balloons to every storm, and it's all for you.

Coming Soon!

Do you need help from Seth and the Rainbow Monsters to #bemoreseth when it comes to the scary changes you can experience in your life?

Book 2, *Don't Be Scared!* is coming soon! Keep an eye on social media and your emails for more information.